Enter

The ANIMAL FAIR

by Alice and Martin Provensen

A Golden Book • New York

Golden Books Publishing Company, Inc., New York, New York 10106

CONTENTS

Stories of Wild Animals

Animals of the Forest

Birds, Fishes, and Other People

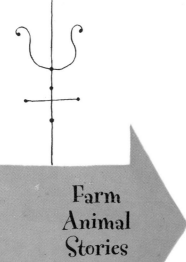

Farm Animal Stories

For Eric and Chris
And now for Richard,
For Karen Anna
And Elizabeth Alice

HOW TO RECOGNIZE A WOLF IN THE FOREST

Wolves are often seen masquerading as someone's grandmother. Here are some things to look for:

A sharp nose

Big, sharp claws

Curly, furry tail

Dainty, pointed ears

Evil, green eyes

Fierce sharp teeth

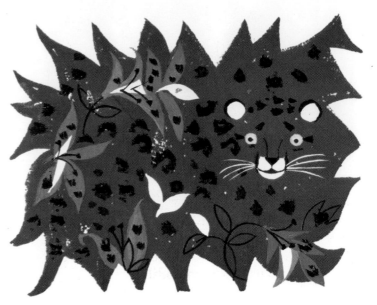

Although the leopard's spots are clear,
they help to make him disappear.

And while the zebra's stripes are bright,
they hide him well in striped light.

Some bugs are quite beyond belief—
the way they hide on twig or leaf.

FLAGE

And this old log—with teeth and smile—
can turn into a crocodile.

But should we try chameleon tricks
for staying out of bed and places,

It isn't apt to work, because—
most people tell *us* by our faces!

All about Birds

ONE DAY a hummingbird sat all by himself on a pole. A sparrow fluttered down and perched beside him. Then a chickadee, a titmouse, a finch, a pipit and other small birds joined them.

"Is something going to happen?" asked a wren.

A little owl looked wise. "I think there's going to be a parade," he said.

A phoebe hurried up. "What's all the excitement?"

"Wait and see," chirped a woodcock.

"This is my place!" screamed a shrike.

"I paid for this seat," squawked a cardinal.

"When are the refreshments going to be served?" asked a little duck.

"I hope it's fish!" said a kingfisher.

"So do I," said a rail.

"I'm sure I must be late!" cried a tern.

Three puffins walked solemnly on the pole. "We have the best seats," they said to each other.

A hawk and a toucan flew up together. "Have a berry while we're waiting," said the hawk politely.

"I'll have one, too," said a stork.

A flamingo remarked to a pelican who had just arrived, "You should wait your turn!"

Then a vulture flapped up. "When do we eat, friends?" he asked with a smile meant to be pleasant.

"Don't speak to me," said a proud eagle. "This seat is reserved. But if you've been invited, I can't stay."

"Who wants their old party," said the vulture in a hurt tone and flapped away.

The pelican looked up in surprise. "Is it over already?" he asked the flamingo.

"Of course," said the stork.

"Then what are we waiting for?" squawked the toucan. And they all flew away together.

"Very enjoyable!" cried the three puffins.

"Most interesting!" said the rail.

"What was it?" asked the woodcock, as he flew after the other birds.

At last only the little hummingbird was left on the pole, and he was sound asleep.

13

The Artist

What's this?

What's that?

I drew a pussy cat!

I'll scare you!

Now who scares who?

A Guessing Game

Who can this be?   Fish from the sea.

Who are you?   Folk from the zoo.

The lion found his mane too warm
One sunny summer day—

And asked the barber in his shop
To snip a mite away.

The barber snipped a mite and said,
"Pray sir, and does that please?"

The lion yawned, "A wee mite more
So I can feel the breeze."

The barber snipped. The lion dozed.
And when he looked again—

He hardly even had a mite
Where once he'd had a mane!

THE CARPENTERS

DEEP in the forest the animals were building a house. But the work lagged.

The beaver ordered everyone about. The fox slept under the tool shed. The chipmunks dropped nuts in the paint pot. The skunk simply sat and combed his tail, and the pack rat stole all the nails.

Just as it began to look as if the house never would be built, a bright blue butterfly came hurrying into the forest.

"A hunter is coming!" she cried.

The fox woke up with a start. The owl fell off his perch. The beaver dove into a pond.

"I knew it would happen!" said the field mouse.

But the sensible fox picked up his saw. "We'll be safe in the house, if we have a house," he said. "Let's get to work!"

The beaver cut logs. The fox sawed them into planks. The chips flew. The beams fell into place and the pack rat brought back all the nails and hammered them in.

The last brick was laid. The last pane of glass was carefully put into the last window. And the door was hung and painted and fitted with a stout lock.

The animals wiped their foreheads and smiled.

"I believe I should have the honor of going in first," said the owl. "I drew the plans."

"I cut the logs," snapped the beaver.

"I drilled the holes," squeaked the field mouse.

"It's my birthday," said the bear.

And there they all stood, arguing at the door, when through the trees, there came the sound of footsteps.

"The hunter!" cried all the animals.

They dove through the windows and down the chimney. Then they slammed the door, turned the key, and waited, shaking with fear.

The footsteps came up the walk.
There was a knock at the door.
"See who it is," whispered the fox.
"No, you," said the possum.
"Not me!" said the squirrel.
"I'll see," said the field mouse. And she peeked out of the keyhole. Then she began to laugh.
"It's a butterfly hunter," she squeaked. "There's nothing to be afraid of."
The animals invited the hunter in.
"I think we should have a party," said the bear. "It's my birthday."
And for once they all agreed.

FRIENDSHIP

Once a wily young flounder named Fish
Said, "Now sinkers-and-bait is my dish!
   But the hooks are the catch
   And a very fine batch
Of bait without hooks is my wish!"

So he said to a lobster he knew,
"Sir, your claws are a wonderful clew!
   Please just snip off these hooks
   And we'll both be the cooks
And the diners on sinker-bait stew."

Now the lobster, I'm happy to state,
Was also most fond of fresh bait.
   With his handy claw-pliers,
   He snipped off the wires
And Fish caught the bait on a plate.

Then he clapped all his fins in great glee,
While the lobster kept laughing, "Tee-hee!"
   And up on the shore
   The fishermen swore
And had to eat corks with their tea!

21

PERSONALITIES

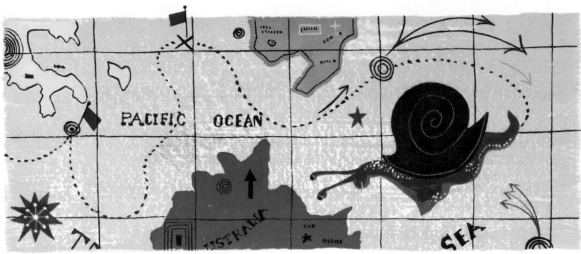

hey say the snail is very slow, but who knows where he wants to go?

rave as a lion's just a phrase, for even he has his quiet days.

f you believe the fox is quick, just try him on arithmetic.

Dumb as an ox, the saying goes, but is he telling all he knows?

The wolf is known as a hungry beast, but he goes for days without a feast.

And though the owl is known as wise, he's never won a spelling prize.

THE ANIMAL FAIR

Here is a farm in the country.
How quiet it seems!

Where is the plough horse?

Where are the spotted cows and the big, brown bull?

Where are the funny goats with yellow eyes and the fat pigs with curly tails?

Where are the ducks with orange bills?

Where is the rooster? And why isn't he crowing?

Where are the farmer and his wife, and most important of all,

Where are the children?

Where? Where? Where? Why the answer is simple. They have all gone to the county animal fair.

Only the hired man is here, sawing logs.

Only the hired girl is here, weeding the flower garden.

Only two sheep and a baby lamb are here, nibbling at the clover.

Only the watch dog is here, chasing cats in a field of rye.

Who else is here?

Who? Why, the crows are here, watching from the woods.

Who else?

The stealthy mice are in the wheat.

A fat raccoon and his wife are eating the tomatoes.

The woodchucks are nibbling the tender asparagus tips.

And as for the greedy rabbits—they started breakfast at one end of the vegetable garden and won't finish supper until they've eaten their way to the other end.

So the quiet farm in the country is not as quiet as it seems.

Here is the animal fair.

You can hear the music of the merry-go-round, and overhead the Ferris wheel turns like a windmill.

Here is the horse. Here are the cows, the chickens, the ducks, and all the other animals. They are scrubbed and brushed, even the pigs, and their faces are shining.

Here are the farmer and his wife. And most important of all, here are the children, running all over the animal fair.

The rooster struts in his stall. "You were foolish to come," he crows to the other birds. "I will win all of the ribbons and all of the medals!"

"Oh, I don't know," honks a goose. "You have a splendid comb, but aren't your legs a little thin?"

The ducks quack with laughter.

"Red wattles! Red wattles!" gobble the turkeys all together. "They will win the prize!"

The mother pig looks fondly at her six little piglets. "The little darlings! Who has more beautiful children?" she sighs.

Only the sheep have nothing to say. They are too busy eating sweet clover to pay any attention to the animal fair.

Now a trumpet sounds and the judges announce the prizes. Everyone stops to listen.

"First Prize—to the first little piglet!"

"Second Prize—to the second little piglet!"

"Third Prize—to the third little piglet!"

And all the other little piglets win little gold medals.

The sheep win a silver cup as big as a milk can.

The farmer puts all his animals into his big truck, and with his wife and children, drives back to the farm. They are tired and happy.

But the rooster is very quiet. "Piglets," he sniffs. "There must be some mistake!"

"Welcome home!" barks the watch dog. "I've guarded the farm."

But wait until morning. Wait until the farmer's wife sees what the rabbits have done to the vegetable garden!

In the Spring

Four young goats on the green spring hill
Skipping and leaping wherever they will,
Rolling themselves in the close-cropped grass,
Butting at shadows of clouds that pass,

Or suddenly, at the skylark's song,
For half a second or half that long,
They lift their heads on the green spring hill—
And they and the hour and the year stand still.

THE VISITORS

ON THE edge of a factory town lived two children. Their yard was paved with cinders. The smoke from the tall chimneys filled the sky over their heads. At night, the light from the furnaces lit their bedroom with a pink glare.

Then they would open their picture books and look at the green fields and the white clouds. But most of all they loved the animals pictured there.

"How nice it would be to play with them," the children thought.

"Would you really like to come and play with us?" said a deep sad voice.

There in the window was the great, shaggy head of a lion with round, yellow eyes.

"Don't be afraid," the lion said. "My friends and I would be delighted to have your company."

The children crept to the window and looked out on the yard. There sat a tiger, a wolf, and a tall red bird. These were the lion's friends.

But they looked so kind and smiled so nicely that the children were not in the least afraid. They jumped down into the yard.

"Climb on our backs," the animals said.

They padded softly past the tall, black chimneys, through streets lined with mean little houses. They went through a gate and over rows and rows of railroad tracks. They crossed a bridge and came to a small blue door in a yellow brick wall. The lion pushed it gently open with his nose and they slipped through.

The children opened their eyes very wide.

The sky was clear. The air was sweet. The golden fields shimmered in the warm sun. And everywhere the children looked were animals. Their picture books had never shown them anything half so beautiful.

The children ran through the fields and laughed out loud. And all the animals laughed with them.

A little bear brought them a honeycomb to eat and a peacock gave them each a beautiful feather from his tail.

"I've plenty more," he said.

They played for hours until at last they fell asleep beside a little brook.

"It's the pleasantest place in the world," they thought dreamily. "If only we could always stay."

But when the children awoke, they were back in their beds. Outside the window, the chimneys sent a shower of sparks high in the air.

"Do you suppose we were dreaming?" the children said.

But there on the floor beside each bed was a peacock feather.

The Warthog

The warthog's face is a disgrace,
His shape is like a jar,
He's never welcome any place,
Where well-dressed people are.

But look at him with kindly eyes,
And you will find, I'm told,
That though he'll win no beauty prize,
His heart is purest gold.

The Mysterious STRANGER

"Good gracious," snorted the horse.

"Land sakes alive," cried the pig.

"What in the world is it?" asked the rooster.

The animals stood in the barn staring in amazement at the new arrival.

"Maybe it's a bull," said the cow doubtfully.

The horse laughed. "Who ever saw a green bull?"

"What's all the excitement about?" asked the little duck. "It's clear that it's a fish. I've often seen fish with eyes like that in the mud at the bottom of the pond."

"No, no. It must be a goose," said a goose. "I heard it honk when it came into the barn."

All the animals began talking at once.

The duck smiled and said, "Anyone can see that it's a fish. If you will listen quietly for a moment, I will explain.

"It's green, isn't it?" he continued.

The animals had to agree.

"It has no legs, has it?"

No, they saw it had no legs, nor feet, nor toes.

"It has big, flat eyes, hasn't it?"

Everyone could see that.

"Well, then," concluded the duck triumphantly, "what else could it be but a fish?" And he waddled off, satisfied that he had solved the mystery.

But the other animals weren't satisfied at all. They wandered about the barnyard mumbling to themselves.

"If it's a fish," muttered the horse, "why doesn't it swim?"

"If it's a fish," grunted the pig, "why is it in the barn?"

"It couldn't possibly be a fish," complained the other animals. "It isn't fishy at all."

After lunch, the farmer, his wife and their three children came out of the house and went into the barn.

36

What a choking and wheezing!

What a grinding and rasping!

Out of the barn roared the mysterious stranger, carrying the farmer and his family.

It hurled itself across the barnyard.

It crashed through the orchard and plunged headlong into the pond.

The farmer, the farmer's wife, and the three children waded to the shore, walked into the farmhouse and closed the door.

The animals were awed.

"What a splash!" said the horse. "I must confess I had a moment of panic."

"You ran like a rabbit," laughed the rooster.

"Is that so?" said the horse. "I didn't see you standing around either, my friend."

Up went the rooster's feathers. The horse bared his teeth.

But just then the little duck came paddling up.

"Are you convinced now?" he asked. "As fine a fish as I've ever seen."

"He's right," said the cow. "It's in the water, that's plain."

"It shows no sign of coming out either," agreed the pig.

"A fish it is," said the rooster solemnly, "and a very dangerous one. How fortunate we are that it's out of our barn."

"Indeed we are!" cried all the animals, hurrying off to see if supper was ready.

And the stranger, up to its engine in water, sat quietly in the pond, while all the fish, both big and little, wondered what in the world it could be.

UNHAPPY
Birthday Party

I've sent out invitations,
To each and every friend.
I've even asked relations,
But no one can attend.

The badger's very busy,
It seems his mother's ill.
The goat is feeling dizzy,
The bush pig has a chill.

The antelope has been mislaid,
The mouse is visiting a rat.
It couldn't be that they're afraid
Of one poor tiger cat!

STORIES
WITHOUT
WORDS

The Runaways

I T WAS the toucan who started all the trouble. . . . He was tired of his wire cage. He was tired of all the people with balloons. "I'm surprised we put up with it," he said.

"Put up with what?" asked the flamingo, who had

been busy admiring his reflection in the drinking pan.

"Oh, I don't know," sighed the toucan. "We never get to go anywhere."

The lion, who had been quietly enjoying the warm sunshine, cocked a furry ear. "That's true," he said.

"All these people visit us, but we never visit anyone."

The elephant, who had been busily eating peanuts, waved his trunk. "I'd like to ride on a street car," he said.

And the bears, in their cage, nodded eagerly.

By feeding time, everyone was so upset that no one had the least appetite for supper. The keepers in the zoo noticed that something was wrong.

Instead of balancing fish on their noses and diving beautifully into their tank, the seals barked coldly and turned their backs.

"What's the matter with the seals?" said the people.

And the elephant would not eat his hay. He only blew it around in his pen in a halfhearted way, and didn't even wave his trunk for peanuts.

"What's the matter with the elephant?" the people asked.

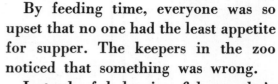

And the lions! No one had ever seen them without an appetite. But they sat with their eyes closed, and when the wagon came around, they didn't even look up.

"What's the matter with the lions?" everyone said.

The keepers cried with vexation.

"What's to be done?" they wept.

But the toucan, who is a clever bird,

was watching his chance.

When the head keeper walked by, the

toucan reached out with his enormous

bill, and lightly took the keys from the

keeper's pocket.

Then he waited quietly until closing

time. He opened his cage, and out he

walked. Next he opened the chimpan-

zee's cage.

And together, they let

all the animals free!

Out of the gates of the zoo rushed the animals. They hurried into the streets of the town.

What a commotion!

The policemen blew their whistles. The street-car conductor clanged his bell and the traffic ran the wrong way. The people rushed in all directions. And sirens blew!

At first the animals enjoyed the excitement. But they soon became a little bewildered.

"What a racket!" said a dainty antelope.

"Is it always as noisy as this?" trumpeted the elephant.

"How dusty the streets are!" said the gnu. "The lights are blinding! I'm a nervous wreck."

"Dear me," sighed the lion. "People seem more friendly when they come to visit us at the zoo."

"Let's go home," snuffled the camel. "I'm tired and hungry." And he started off.

The other animals hesitated for only a moment. Then they followed him back to the zoo.

"How peaceful!" said the bear, as he crept into his cage. "I don't really care for the city."

"Neither do I!" said the elephant.

The lion stretched out in his den with a contented sigh. "There's no place like home," he said.

But the toucan didn't say anything, because he hadn't come back. He was on his way to South America.

Pretending

I have quite a handy habit. When I hurry—I'm a rabbit.

When I'm buying chops and stew, I'm a tiger—hungry, too!

When I meet a friendly horse, I'm another horse, of course.

If you run and try to catch me, I will vanish in the air.

And before you finish blinking—I'm a most surprising bear.

So if when you go out walking, there's a fox behind a tree—

Don't be afraid and call for aid—it's probably only me.

THE REFORMED FOX

ONE DAY while the farmer was away, a fox walked boldly into the barnyard. The hens ran cackling this way and that. The ducks jumped up and down and clacked their bills. And the geese hissed angrily from under the haystack.

But the fox sat quietly in the center of the barn-

yard. Then he smiled and said, "My dears, I know how you feel about foxes, but it is lonely in the forest. I would like to come and live with you as a friend. Would you help me to reform?"

"Certainly not," said the rooster.

"What an idea!" said the goose. And all the ducks and chickens looked suspiciously at the fox.

But the horse was deeply moved. "Poor fellow," he said.

A tear trickled down the cow's soft nose.

"We might let him stay for today," said the pig.

The fox smiled sweetly and chucked the little chicks under the chin. "I will be as good as gold," he said. And he was.

He learned his barnyard lessons well.

"How handsome you all are," said the fox as he learned to walk in the goose step.

"Oh, yes," said the geese. "We're the finest people in the barnyard."

"I quite agree," said the fox.

The rooster was still suspicious. He followed the fox everywhere at a safe distance.

"He still looks foxy to me," he crowed.

"What a beautiful voice you have," said the fox. "Do you suppose you could find time to teach me to sing?"

The rooster ruffled his feathers with pride.

And when the fox took lessons in hatching eggs, all the chickens were thrilled.

The fox took especially good care of the ducklings. He smoothed their feathers and wiped their noses. He led them down the winding path to the millpond. It was a charming sight to see them splashing together.

"What delightful children you have!" said the fox to the mother duck. "And they swim so gracefully."

"It's sweet of you to say so, Fox dear," she replied.

The goat gave the fox lessons in self defense. "For butting is certainly the most useful thing to know," he said.

Soon all the farm animals were clamoring for Fox's attention. How popular he was! The pig invited him to share his supper and the horse offered to share his stall.

"You have all been so very kind," said the fox. "I wish I could repay you. Do you like strawberries?"

"Oh, yes," said the goat.

"Delightful!" said the pig.

"Well," said the fox, "I know of a wonderful berry patch on the edge of the forest. Why don't we have a picnic supper?"

"I'm very fond of picnics," said the goose.

"Let's all go!" said the cow.

How happy the ducklings were, for they dearly loved an outing.

And off they went through the fields.

What an odd procession it was! The fox led the way. Next came the ducks in single file. After them waddled the geese. Then came the rooster and his big family, bringing up the rear.

Just at that moment the farmer drove into the barnyard. He looked around in great surprise.

"Where are all the chickens?" said the farmer's wife.

"Where are the ducks and the geese?" cried the farmer.

"There they are," barked the dog. "A fox has got them!" And he raced into the field.

"Why, there is the farmer," cried all the picnickers. "And here comes Dog. He wants to go picnicking too."

The fox took one quick look and decided not to try to explain. He slipped into the forest with the dog yelping at his black heels. Presently the dog came limping back.

"You have spoiled our picnic," cried the duckling.

The geese hissed, "Silly oaf! Now we shall have no strawberries!"

And they all turned and walked back to the barnyard where the farmer's wife gave them a terrible scolding.

Deep in the forest sat the fox. "Drat!" he said. "Not even one little duckling." And he gnashed his sharp teeth in a great rage.

Said a bird who was learning to fly,
To a lofty giraffe passing by,
"Do you think it quite fair,
To be there in the air,
Without even having to try?"

TALL
AND SMALL

Said an ant on the leaf of a plant,
To a rhino, "You may rave and rant,
But on your hide I'll roam,
And there make a home,
For my sisters and cousins and aunt."

54

LITTLE AND
BIG

In the Fall

I walk on yellow leaves in fall,
And see the earth from summer turning.

I hear the brown birds' distant call,
And smell the autumn fires burning.

Soon all the leaves will fade and die,
The last wild birds will rise and roam.

The wind will blow and snow will fly,
But I'll be warm and safe at home.

Find a comfortable cave.

Make sure it is vacant.

Lay in a good supply of fire wood.

Stock up on goodies for snacks.

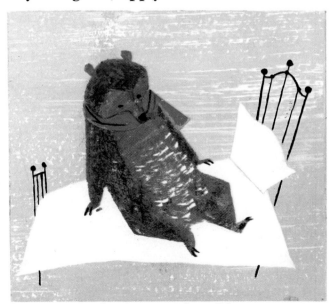

Be sure the bed is comfortable.

Set the clock for spring.

How to Sleep Through the Winter *(Hibernate)*